TALES FROM THE CHICKEN YARD
AND OTHER FOWL STORIES

COCK A DOODLE DOOOOO

BY

ELIZABETH DETTLING MORENO

ISBN-13: 978-1-970079-26-5

Library of Congress Control Number:

Printed in the United States of America

Illustrated by Jeanette Crum

Published and Edited by:

Opportune Independent Publishing Co.
113 N. Live Oak Street
Houston, TX 77003
(832) 263-1700
www.opportunepublishing.com

Dedication

With a grateful heart,

I dedicate this

To my Parents,

John Louis and Geraldine Wendel Dettling,

Who instilled in me

A love for nature,

Especially Chickens.

Dad was a story teller

And mom was the Rock we all depended on.

Thank you, Mom and Dad!

You are loved

And you are missed.

Additional appreciation to

Jeanette Smaistrla Crum

For accepting the challenge

To illustrate this book.

(It only took 14 years to find her!)

Thank you!!!

You are a blessing!

Table of Contents

Prologue

"It all happened so fast!" lamented Miss Lizzy. "I can't believe she's gone and now we have all these pups to care for! Who would have ever thought we'd have **dognappers** in our neighborhood?! I thought we'd be safe in this *rural* area."

"Yes, Lizzy," agreed Farmer Gabe, "even here in the country, we're not as safe as we thought we'd be. She must have known there was someone out there who was up to no good when she was doing all that barking.

I should have never let her out until I went with her to see what was going on. How will we ever tell George and Marianne that their best dog was stolen today? We promised we would take care of her and the pups till they got back from their vacation tour of Texas. They started off in Padre Island at the beach just three days ago and news like this could ruin their trip."

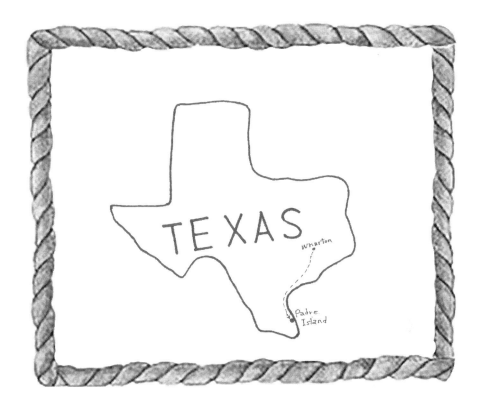

"Honey, you didn't know what was goin' on, so don't you go blaming yourself. Things like this happen," his wife added. "We'll find a way to take care of those six little rascals. It's a good thing they're already weaned or else we would really be in trouble. Since they can eat solid food, it won't be quite so bad as if we had to bottle feed them and it's a good thing their Grandma Noel is here to keep an eye on them. She'll make them behave. After all, she was such a good mother to her litter of pups and they all turned out all right. In fact, Sugar was the best pup out of all."

"You are right about that. Let's get Junior to make up

some posters to hang up around town and then put an ad in the paper," the farmer suggested. "It might be like looking for a **needle in a haystack**, but it is worth a try. Maybe somebody somewhere will know where she is. We might be able to get her back if we offer a big enough reward."

"Well, we've got to do something and that's a good place to start," Miss Lizzy *interjected*. "I'll go get him right now."

"Hold on a minute, little lady," said Farmer Gabe. "We forgot the most important thing of all."

"And, *pray tell*, what is that?" questioned his wife.

"To pray about her safety and her safe return," he answered.

So the two held hands and prayed and *committed* Sugar to the Lord's care. Then they thanked Him in advance for whatever the outcome would be.

Next, they moved the pups to the back yard and put Noel in the pen with them. She was *reluctant* because she was used to staying in the comfortable house, but when she saw her confused litter of grandchildren, she softened and decided to do her best to help out in this crisis situation.

With that, the family began a new adventure and Noel became the best storyteller around on "God's Little Acre."

Psalm 26:7, KJV

That I may **publish** with the voice of thanksgiving and tell of all thy wondrous works.

"Noel" Tells Tales from the Chicken Yard

"Children, come here," instructed Grandma Noel. "I need to talk to you about something very important."

"Aw, Grandma, why did we have to be put in this pen anyway? I was having fun running after that butterfly," yelped Barker.

"And I wanted to go chase the cows," complained Cowboy.

"Why did I have to wake up from my nap?" asked Midnight Star. "You know I need my beauty rest."

"Grandma, can't Bingo and I go play before supper?" added Punkin. "We promise not to get dirty."

Teddy Bear came running in late because he had been out riding on the tractor with Farmer Gabe. "What's going on?" he asked breathlessly.

"Little ones, I have sad news for you and I need for you to pay close attention. Listen to me very carefully," *admonished* their grandma. "Your mother is missing, and I will be having to take care of you until she returns or until George and Marianne come back to take you home."

Suddenly, the pups were all ears as they realized the full impact of what Noel had told them. Their beloved mommy and Grandma Noel's favorite daughter would not be on the farm to help take care of them and might not ever come back unless God answered their prayers. Noel very carefully explained what had happened and how important it was for them to behave during this crisis and she assured them that no matter how long it took, the people would not give up hope of finding their son and daughter-in- law's dog Sugar.

As the puppies whimpered and cried, Noel knew she would have to do something to get their minds off the problem, so she thought of a plan of action. She would entertain them with stories about the critters that lived on their farm and she began by telling them about herself and all kinds of tales from the chicken yard. And here begins her story…

"Little ones, sometimes Farmer Gabe and Miss Lizzy seem to think that I just might be part human because I amaze them with my outstanding abilities. I tend to think I was born gifted that way and so was your Grandpa Balkie. I do believe your momma is gifted like that, too."

"Grandpa Balkie, rest his soul, thought he was supposed to be the guardian angel for Miss Lizzy. He followed that woman all around like he was stuck to her like glue. You would have liked him because he was such a *character*. I miss him so since his accident. Such a shame that he died while taking care of Miss Lizzy."

"Your grandpa Balkie was part Chihuahua and part toy poodle, so he was just my size. We had such good times together! Some of you pups look so much like him it just blesses my heart. Cowboy, honey, you are so much like him that it seems he's here with me all over again. And, Teddy Bear, you're the *spittin' image* of him and you like riding

18

around on the tractor just like he did."

"Grandma," exclaimed the kids. "Tell us more about Grandpa. What was he like? Did he ever chase rabbits? What kinds of games did he like to play? Did he ever chase cats?"

"Oh, goodness, I could tell you so much about Grandpa, but there's other things I need to tell you first. I'll tell you about him later, but since you are on this farm for just a little while, I need to tell you about the chickens and animals that live here with us," Noel told her grandpups.

"Before I start the stories about these chickens, I have to tell you a story about me first," said Noel very matter-of-factly. "You see, I was healed once upon a time from a broken back. Why, I was so bad off that I could barely move my body out of my bed to take a walk.

"Why, Grandma! What did you do? How did you take care of yourself?" asked Punkin.

"It was all I could do to move my two front legs and drag the rest of my body away from my comfortable bed. Miss Lizzy took me to Doctor Chapman, the veterinarian, and he was really sympathetic, don't you know? He took an x-ray and was so sad when he told Miss Lizzy that we would decide what to do with me after a few weeks. He didn't come right out and say it, but it kind of sounded like he wanted to put me out of pain completely by putting me to sleep, now and forever! Well, *euthanasia* was out of the question for me as far as Miss Lizzy was concerned, but she was indeed *perplexed*."

"Grandma," asked Bingo, "weren't you scared? Were you afraid you might die?"

"Well, sweetie, I was feelin' so low that I thought it might happen, but something else happened instead.

Miss Trisha, another lady in the clinic, heard the *prognosis*, so she asked Miss Lizzy if she believed in praying. Why, Miss Lizzy was shocked because she was always the one asking other people if they would like to pray. Of course, she accepted Miss Trisha's offer and the two of them prayed right there in the doctor's office and asked the good Lord in Heaven to have mercy on me and heal me, in Jesus' name."

"Did you get better right away, Grandma? Did you, did you?" now Barker was asking the questions. Cowboy joined in, "Grandma, tell us what happened next."

Noel continued her story. "It wasn't *instantaneous* by any means, but I am here to tell you that the touch of God is on my life. About four weeks later, you could see me running figure eights all over the yard and just rejoicing 'cause God was soooooo good to me."

"Grandma, is that why you tell us things about God all the time? You must love Him a lot!" Bingo started figuring the whole thing out.

"Oh, Grandma, I never knew you had been so sick," whispered Midnight Star. "I'm so glad He made you well."

"Now, pups, I want you to know that if God cared enough to heal me from the injury in my back, He cares enough to keep His eye on your mamma so she comes back safely, too." Noel continued her story.

"I've got another story to tell you now and it's the story

of how Farmer Gabe, Miss Lizzy, Junior, and I came to live on this farm," said Grandma Noel.

"But Grandma," Cowboy asked, "haven't you always lived here? I LOVE this place! And especially chasing the cows next door."

"Well," Grandma replied, "it's like this—Farmer Gabe and Miss Lizzy took me from my quiet little neighborhood in the city to a farm with all kinds of chickens and fine feathered friends. I knew something was up because they would take me for rides in the car …"

Teddy Bear interrupted, "I like riding in cars, too!"

"Sweetie, you're being rude. Let Grandma finish, then you can tell me what you have to say. Anyway, we'd drive to the *rural* area outside of town, then they would stop outside of a fenced in yard and just look and look at this old farmhouse, kind of like a puppy salivating over a doggie treat."

"What's salivating?" asked Bingo.

"You know how when you get hungry all that wet spit starts piling up and dripping from your mouth? That is what it means to salivate," Noel explained. "These little episodes went on for weeks and weeks, then one day they started acting crazy filling up boxes and putting everything they owned on pick-up trucks and took it to that little acre that they had been drooling over."

"And that's how you became a farm dog, right, Grandma?" Barker and Punkin asked at the same time.

"Yes, that's exactly right. Before I knew it, I was witness to more *shenanigans* and carryings on than I would have ever imagined coming from the chicken yard. I minded my own business the best I could, but I couldn't help but notice that things were sure different around here."

Noel concluded her story, then *admonished* the young ones, "Now, you remember what I said about God taking care of your momma, and taking care of you, too. That's all the storytelling for today, but I'll have another one for you tomorrow. And if you are really good, I might just have two."

The puppies yelped playfully as Noel got up from her rug and they ran figure eights around her just for the fun of it, knowing that God was taking care of their whole family and especially, Sugar, their mom.

Jeremiah 29:11, KJV

For I know the thoughts that I think toward you, saith the LORD, thoughts of peace, and not of evil, to give you an expected end.

That Bad Rooster!

Farmer Gabe, Miss Lizzy, **his better half**, and their son Junior lived near Wharton, a small country town on the Texas Gulf Coast, **just a hop, skip, and a jump** from the beach at Matagorda. They were caring for their son and daughter-in-law's dog, Sugar, and her six pups while the young couple went on a two-week vacation to tour Texas. On the third day of the dog's visit, someone stole Sugar from the front yard of the farmhouse. The family tried everything they could think of to find the lost dog, but they were not sure where to begin. George and Marianne had already gone to Laredo and now were in the Big Bend Country, so Farmer Gabe and Miss Lizzy didn't want to ruin their trip with the news of Sugar being dognapped. Noel, their little terrier dog, was Sugar's mother, so she was elected to care for her grandpups.

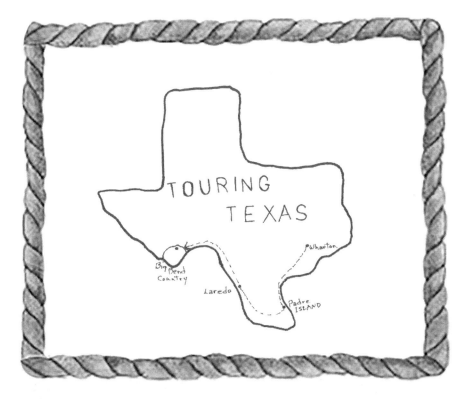

It was the first day after Sugar was taken and as nighttime drew near, the puppies were showing signs of missing her. Farmer Gabe and Miss Lizzy had taken Junior's posters to hang up around town and Junior was scanning the neighborhood to see if he could find any signs of her whereabouts. As always, Noel came to the rescue and gathered the little ones together under the oak tree in the back yard.

"When's mommy coming back?" asked Barker and
Teddy Bear. "We miss playing chase with her."

"Yeah, when will she be here? I need her to help me get
these stickers out of my fur," added Punkin. Midnight Star
chimed in, "I miss taking my nap on her soft warm neck."

Cowboy just chewed on an old worn out shoe to take out his frustration. All the pups became very thoughtful and moaned softly. Then Bingo broke the silence. "Do you think the people are still praying for her to come back? Do you think she really is okay?"

Grandma Noel was silent for a minute herself, then said, "Little ones, we don't know when your mom will come back, or even if she will. But I know that Farmer Gabe and Miss Lizzy haven't given up on her. I heard them praying for her again just before they left. So we'll just have to keep trusting the good Lord for whatever the outcome is. But you know what? Now is a really good time for that story I promised you yesterday."

All the pups yelped together. "Grandma, we love your stories! What are you going to tell us about this time?"

Grandma thought and thought, then announced, "You pups need a good laugh, so tonight I'm going to tell you about one really bad rooster. He was always causing mischief around here and his name was Mr. Roo."

Then Grandma Noel began her story. "When we talk about real **characters** around here, that Bad Rooster is at the top of the list. Miss Lizzy called him 'Mr. Roo,' but everybody else called him 'Bad.' He was an old white Leghorn who **had been around the barnyard a few times** before he came to live on our little farm."

"Grandma, does 'Leghorn' mean his leg looks like a horn or that it is a horn?" asked Bingo, the deep thinker.

"Land sakes, no, Bingo. A Leghorn is a skinny chicken or rooster with a long neck. The people say they're so skinny that they're not very good for eating, but the hens are great egg layers. Old Roo had **spurs** that were almost two inches long above his toes and he wasn't afraid to use them. And those bright red things that hung down from under his beak–those are called '**wattles**'—were almost four inches long.

Nobody, and I mean nobody, could come near that rascal without him thinking he had to come spur them. He was so bad that no one walked to the barnyard or anywhere near him without carrying something for protection. There's an old saying that goes *'walk **softly but carry a big stick**.'* Well, that's what Farmer Gabe and Miss Lizzy and Junior did around him and with just cause."

"Did he ever get you, Grandma? I'll bet I could have chased him and scared him, too!" laughed Barker.

Cowboy agreed. "Yeah, Grandma, we would have had him running."

"Now, boys," Noel chided. "You are talking brave now, but Roo really was bad. Yes, he did chase me a few times, but

I made sure I was with Miss Lizzy or Farmer Gabe when I went out there and they always carried something to hit him with just in case he started acting up.

Old Roo had a glint in his eye that said he was looking for trouble. His beak was kind of off-center, like a snarl. He looked kind of like a fighter who had battle scars from his challenges. That bad rooster strutted around like he owned the place and crowed proudly to let everyone know he was in charge. The people didn't trust him and I didn't either!"

"You're too young to know how people celebrate the New Year but, Mr. Roo must have known a new year was happening the first year we were on the farm because as soon as the clock struck twelve midnight, that bad boy started crowing and crowing and crowing, for at least ten minutes… almost like he was welcoming the new year too. He must have known we were changing from 1999 to 2000 and that made the New Year even more special.

And when he was done, he was quiet again, till dawn."

Midnight Star was puzzled. "What is twelve midnight? What happens then? Why was it a new year?"

Noel quickly explained that twelve midnight is when one day changes to the next day and that a new year was when one year changed to the next one. The answer satisfied the pup.

Grandma continued her story.

"Another time, Mr. Roo got concerned because there was a lunar eclipse. Oh, I see this is another thing I need to explain. A lunar eclipse happens at night every once in a while, when the shadow of the sun comes between the earth and the moon and the moon gets dark for a while. He couldn't figure out where the moon went, so he did his crowing routine again about ten o'clock at night until the moon came out from the shadows. You would have thought he was the one who was responsible for the sun, moon, and stars by the way he did his crowing that night."

"I thought chickens slept at night, Grandma," said

Teddy Bear.

"Most of the time, they do," chuckled Noel. "But those were two times Roo was more concerned with astronomy than he was with a good night's rest.

She had more to tell about that wicked critter. Noel went on to the next phase of his escapades. "That Bad Rooster scared Farmer Gabe, although he didn't take any foolishness from that crazy bird. But my Miss Lizzy liked the scoundrel because she thought he had personality. Anyway, one day Farmer Gabe was going to check on the critters and Roo came out of nowhere trying to catch him off guard. Before he knew what hit him, Farmer Gabe had whacked that loony Leghorn with a stick. That was just about the funniest thing I ever saw because that rooster let out a sick sounding squawk and fell to the ground, probably seeing stars and planets orbiting around him."

"Grandma, did he look like those chickens in the cartoons? You know the ones that always get hurt, then they see things floating above them? I'll bet he looked silly!" Cowboy knew exactly what Grandma was talking about.

"Yes, baby, he sure did look woozy, but I kind of felt sorry for him.

Farmer Gabe just knew he was in trouble because the Bad Rooster was at *death's doorstep*. He looked at the rooster, then he thought what Miss Lizzy would say, then he looked at the rooster again, and he started pleading, 'Rooster, don't die! Please don't die, Rooster!' Well, a few minutes later, that crazy bird squawked again and swooned as he stood up."

"Was he good then, Grandma?" the curious pups wanted to know, "Did he stop being mean to everybody? What happened to him after that?"

"Well," Grandma chuckled, "before long he was back to causing mischief. He did kind of hold back a little more than before, but I don't think he ever did learn his lesson. Roo's reign of terror lasted less than two years because his little boy roosters grew into big boy roosters and they did their best to *upset his apple cart*. Once they became teenagers, they started giving him *a taste of his own medicine* and he didn't like it one single bit! He tried to maintain control, but his age was catching up with him and he just couldn't handle the problems his young uns gave him."

"If he was so mean, Grandma, then that served him right!" all the pups barked in unison. "Were his children as bad as he was?"

Grandma finished her story. "Well, they weren't mean to the people. They just took over the chicken yard and Roo drifted away, *like an old Eskimo going to the polar bears*. One day Miss Lizzy came to feed the flock and Roo was nowhere around. All she found was a few loose white feathers floating outside of the chicken yard. And don't you know she treasured those memories of that unforgettable, *bodacious* Bad Rooster. But now, it's time for good little puppies to go to sleep, so good night, sleep tight, and I'll see you in the morning."

Proverbs 16:18, KJV

Pride goeth before destruction,
and a haughty spirit before a fall.

Princess, The Dignified Hen

George and Marianne had no idea of the drama taking place at George's parent's house while they traveled around Texas. They were still in the Big Bend country but getting ready to move on for a day or two in the Texas Panhandle where they were going to watch the musical at the Palo Duro

State Park. They had left Sugar, their small dog, and all of her young pups with Farmer Gabe and Miss Lizzy, George's parents, while they went on their Texas vacation. The family was totally dismayed to find that Sugar had been dognapped from their front yard three days after George and Marianne had left. While the farmer and his wife and their son Junior tried to find the little mommy, their own dog, Noel, was taking care of the puppies, which were actually her grandbabies.

It was the third night that Sugar was gone and her babies were restless. Grandma Noel was **plumb tuckered out** after a day of chasing all over the barnyard after them. When Farmer Gabe and Miss Lizzy closed her up in the pen in the back yard with the pups for the night, she was grateful to have a soft pillow to rest her weary bones. She called the grandpups to her and began her next story. Punkin, Cowboy, Bingo, Midge (her nickname for Midnight Star), Teddy Bear, and Barker, come over here with Grandma and listen to a story about a very special chicken," declared Noel. "When Farmer Gabe and Miss Lizzy first moved to our farm, Miss Lizzy knew she wanted some chickens.

So one day, she took the truck with a wire cage in back to the feed store and she came home with a **black crested hen**, two almost grown **guineas**, and one strange looking chicken they called an **Aracauna**. They named the little hen "Princess" because of her crown–that's another name for her crest- and because she carried herself with *dignity.*

"That means she was always sweet and nice and never did anything to cause trouble. She didn't act silly and she always carried her head high, just like a queen," Grandma continued. "Miss Lizzy almost always gave names to the chickens. Don't rightly know why, but she was creative with her ***nomers and misnomers***."

"Princess turned out to be one super deluxe mamma! She sat on nests five or six times a year and hatched out more babies than the people could count. She was as good a mother as I was in my younger days. At one time, she was mother to 12 of her own and foster mother to 12 more that came from the incubator. No sooner would she get a batch of chickees big enough to fend for themselves, that she would begin laying again, then start sitting on her next round of little ones. Since it only takes chicken eggs three weeks to hatch, she would always be contributing to the *fowl population explosion*."

"Grandma, what is an *inki bate er*?" Bingo continued in his quest for knowledge.

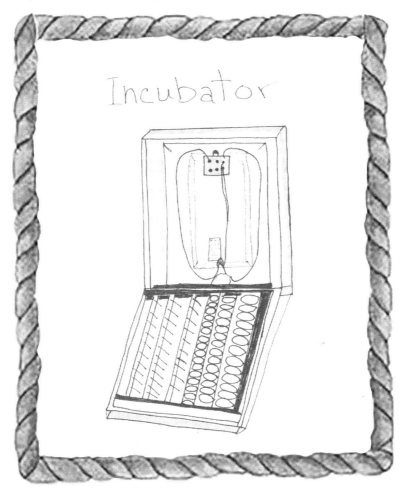

"Ooops! I should have told you that sooner. Did you see that white box Miss Lizzy has in the barn? The one that looks like an ice chest with wires coming out of it? Well, she puts eggs inside of there and the heat keeps them warm, then after a certain amount of time, the eggs hatch out and Miss Lizzy has a new bunch of chicks. That's what an incubator is." Grandma Noel seemed to know the answer to just about every question the young uns could give her.

She resumed telling about Princess. "One time the people got really concerned because they couldn't find their precious little hen. They made such a big to do over her missing. They just **grieved** and **grieved** because their poor little Princess was gone. My goodness, you would have thought it was their pet dog that had died!

If I could have talked, I would have told them where she was, but no one asked me. Anyway, after the twenty-one-day sitting session, Princess showed up in the barn one day with 12 little black shadows under her wing!"

"Why was she gone so long, Grandma? Do you think our mamma is hiding so she can have more babies, too?" Midnight Star seemed much more attentive now that she could compare Princess to her missing mother.

As smart as Noel was, it was hard for her to handle that question, but she accepted it anyway. "For one thing, it takes chickens three weeks or 21 days to hatch their eggs.

For another thing, I know all of you are missing your mom and I am too. I don't think she could be having more babies right now because you boys and girls are still babies. God made dogs so they usually have only two litters of pups a year. But we hope she is somewhere where she can surprise us by coming back one day. Wouldn't that be nice?"

All the pups murmured their agreement.

When the little noises settled down, Noel spoke again to finish her tale.

"Now you know it is almost bedtime, so let me tell you a little more about this hen. There was a time when Princess and all of her babies had a genuine case of chicken pox!"

"Grandma, don't tease us like that!" Barker and Cowboy couldn't see how that could possibly be true.

"No, I'm not *joshin'*," Noel spoke seriously about the situation. "That little hen and all her babies had pimply bumps all over them and they were all so swelled up that their eyes were closed They looked awful and I sure was glad I wasn't a chicken! Miss Lizzy and Farmer Gabe worried that it was contagious and it was... for chickens, but not for people or dogs, thank goodness!"

Punkin and Midge joined in the conversation. "What did Miss Lizzy do for them, Grandma? How long did they look all bumpy and swollen?" The girls could just imagine how they would have looked with a case of the pox.

"Miss Lizzy called Dr. Chapman, the veterinarian, and Old McDonald, the county agent, and both hit the nail on the head when they told her it would run its course in about six weeks, and that was exactly on target. The babies and Princess built up immunities and never would have the pox again."

It was Bingo's turn for another question. "What's '*im mune i tea*'? Is it something good?"

Noel was glad to explain. "Immunity is when you have had something, like a shot, and it keeps you from getting sicker than you would have been if you hadn't had the shot. Like Farmer Gabe makes sure all the big dogs here get rabies shots... it gives them a temporary immunity from rabies, so they can't get it for at least a year. Those little chicks built up an immunity to chicken pox without ever getting a shot or taking medicine."

"Oh," said Bingo, "I think I understand."

"What happened to Princess after that? Why haven't we seen her around the farm anymore?" the pups yapped their queries to their grandma.

Noel *reminisced* about the royal black hen. "I remember the last time I saw Princess.

She was sitting on eggs under an old shoe shine chair in our barn. There weren't many times that she wasn't on a nest, so the people didn't pay her much mind and I didn't either. But that night, when I was safe with Farmer Gabe and

Miss Lizzy and Junior in their house, Princess *gave up the ghost*. A shaggy dog came to our place and had Princess for a midnight snack. All that was left in the morning was a dozen little beige eggs, and a few shiny black feathers."

'Grandma, that's so sad." Midge and Punkin cried. "Why did you tell us something like that before we go to sleep?'

"Yes, I know, it is sad, but I want you to know that memories are strong and as long as a memory remains, a life goes on. And do you know that every time Miss Lizzy and Farmer Gabe look over their flock of chickens, they see the many young chickens that Princess had hatched in her short lifetime? And they see that Princess is still with them, even though she's gone. And now it is time for six little *scamps* to close their eyes for a sweet night of slumber." With that, Noel and the pups settled down for a good night's rest.

Mathews 23:37, KJV
…How often would I have gathered thy children together, even as a hen gathereth her chickens under her wings…

The Hen That Crowed

Farmer Gabe and Miss Lizzy had been searching for Sugar for four days now without any results. Their son, George, and his wife, Marianne were in West Texas between Big Bend and the Panhandle on their two-week tour of Texas. After spending some time at the McDonald National Observatory and Big Bend National Park, they were heading on to the Cadillac Ranch in Amarillo.

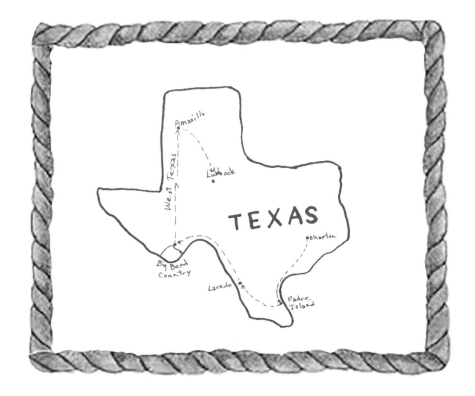

They would return in seven days to take their *canines* home, but they hadn't been told yet that their mother dog had been stolen three days after they left. Noel, the pup's grandma, was a great *surrogate mother*, although she didn't know how long she would have to fill in for her missing daughter. Many prayers went up in Sugar's behalf, but only God knew what the outcome would be.

By the time the fourth day without Sugar rolled around, Noel had the situation with Sugar's pups well in hand. She gave them comfort every day by being right there with them and every night by telling them stories till their tired little eyes closed to end the day. It was a good thing that she was such an intelligent dog because she had more *tricks up her sleeve* for calming the pups than a magician had rabbits in a hat.

This cool summer evening was no exception. Although a gentle gulf breeze was blowing for a change, Farmer Gabe and Miss Lizzy were in the house and Noel and the little ones were rolling in the soft green grass, waiting for the right moment for story time to begin. And then, when the sun had almost gone down like a coin dropped in a piggy bank, the perfect time had arrived. So Noel began her next tale about an unusual chicken on their farm.

"When I first told you about Princess," Noel explained, "I mentioned a very strange looking chicken that Miss Lizzy bought at the same time. This critter was an Araucana, a *descendant* of some tribe of chickens from South America. Miss Lizzy had heard that Araucana are called Easter egg chickens because they laid green or blue colored eggs. She kept waiting for that hen to start laying green eggs because she always thought it would be kind of neat to have real green eggs and ham. Princess was already showing her *fertility*, but the strange bird just kind of existed. Miss Lizzy started calling it 'Arky' because that was the shortest nickname she could think of for an Araucana."

"Farmer Gabe and Miss Lizzy kept looking at the strange one, wondering what was wrong. It had flowing white feathers, but its comb looked all squished together and there didn't seem to be many tail feathers. In spite of its awkwardness, the bird was quite large and ate heartily. All of the others in the flock seemed to be picking on it like the ducks in the 'Ugly Duckling' story.

Even the two guineas had fun *harassing* Arky. They pecked at it and chased it mercilessly. The poor misfit didn't seem to have a friend in the world. But one day, all of that changed."

"I would have been his friend," Teddy Bear said. "I always like to make friends."

"I would have, too," added Bingo. "They shouldn't have been making fun of him. Our mommy taught us to be kind to each other, and that means to animals who are different from us, too."

"Your mommy was right," said Noel. "It is a good thing to be friendly to other people, especially those that don't have friends."

"What happened next, Grandma? Did he start chasing those mean old bullies?" the inquisitive Cowboy and Barker wanted to know.

"Well, this is what happened." Grandma continued her story. "It was evening feeding time and I was protecting Miss Lizzy from Mr. Roo. She was throwing out hands full of cracked corn and chicken scratch when all of a sudden a really weird sound shocked both of us. RRRRRR---OOOOOOO---EEERRRRR. My ears stood up in agony and Miss Lizzy laughed so hard that her sides hurt. She went to get Farmer Gabe so he could hear the *raucous*, too."

"What was the noise, grandma? Was there a strange monster nearby?" one of the pups asked the question that was on everybody's mind.

"No, no, that wasn't it at all. They both shook their heads in disbelief as they watched Arky let loose with another ear-piercing, less than professional crow. He was the one making the weird sounds that made them laugh so hard.

"Now they knew why there were no green eggs... green eggs have to come from a hen, and Arky was most assuredly a male member of the species. It wasn't long after that that he sprouted a beautiful set of tail feathers and could crow with the best of them. He started courting the females that Roo didn't have control of, and before long, those hens were fertile with Arky's offspring.

Noel smiled as she remembered the transformed misfit. "Now, Arky was proud of his tail feathers once they grew out. It was almost like he was laughing at his former tormentors because now he was twice their size and was downright good looking, to boot."

"I'll bet he could beat up the others now, couldn't he, Grandma?"

"Yes, child, he could have, but he chose not to unless some other rooster or the **guineas** came into his territory. Then he reminded them that they didn't belong there by chasing them like you pups would, but he never did hurt anyone."

Well, one hot summer afternoon, Arky had a major crisis. A stray cow-dog had taken up residence in the neighbor's pasture and he thought it was a help-yourself-buffet in our back pasture with quite a selection of poultry to choose from. He dined from our flock once or twice a week, even though I chased him away every time I saw him."

"Grandma, I like to chase cows. Does that make me a cow-dog, too?" Cowboy didn't want to be as disliked as that dog was.

"Sweetie, you might be a little cow-dog, but you could never be as evil as he was. Some dogs are raised just for taking care of cows, so they call them 'cow-dogs.' He was one of those. I think he was a blue healer because he had gray hide and brown and black spots all over him. And he loved to be with the cows, even more than he liked to be with people."

"We would have chased him, too, if we had been there." Cowboy and Barker added their two cents worth. "Then what happened?"

Noel thought back to that hot afternoon a couple of summers ago. She resumed her story. "That particular afternoon, Miss Lizzy was running behind schedule and I was taking a nap in the people house. When Miss Lizzy got to the silver chicken pen, she found Arky squawking loudly for help just as that mongrel was trying to carry him off, *lock, stock, and barrel*. That woman went runnin' and screamin' and throwin' things and finally convinced the culprit to let go of her prize rooster. The devil dog let go, all right, but not before he took out every last feather out of Arky's backside and left nothing but a naked tail. Talk about embarrassed! That poor Araucana went into hiding like ***King David's men after their beards were cut off***. It took weeks and weeks, but finally, he was able to face the flock. That encounter was just too close for comfort!"

"How awful!" said the Punkin and Midge. "He must have been glad when his tail finally grew back."

"He certainly was, you can be sure. And he was so glad to be in charge of the hen house again. He really did have something to crow about then!" Then, all of a sudden, Noel grew quiet and her eyes misted over for a second.

"Children," she spoke solemnly, "I regret to tell you that the rascal eventually did make off with Arky and Miss Lizzy wasn't around to save him. Someone forgot to shut the gate on the chicken pen one night in the fall and that was all the invitation that the wicked cowdog needed. Arky, the kingly Araucana, was gone for good."

"Grandma, you told us another sad story," the pups cried in unison.

"Well, your mom might have told you a *Bible* verse that we heard Miss Lizzy and Farmer Gabe talk about from time to time. Something like when the devil means something for harm, God can turn it around and make something good out of it. That's what He did for Arky."

"How could anything good come out of his dying, Grandma?" the pups were *perplexed*, but needed an answer.

"Well, it took a while, but Arky's children grew up and sure enough, there were some hens and they did indeed lay green eggs. Miss Lizzy was so excited when she found the first ones that she had to show them off to anyone who would halfway listen. So, in spite of what was meant for evil, things did turn out for good and Miss Lizzy and her friends and family are enjoying her green eggs, usually without ham."

Psalm 127:3, KJV

Lo, children are an heritage of the LORD:
and the fruit of the womb is his reward.

Saddleback, Arky's Son

Farmer Gabe and Miss Lizzy became more frustrated as they were unable to find their son's dog, Sugar. While they were dog-sitting the pets for their son and his wife, the mamma dog, Sugar, had been stolen from their front yard. They were left with six little pups to care for, with the help of their part terrier dog, Noel, who was also Sugar's mother. The family distributed posters and put ads everywhere, but it was like looking for a *needle in a haystack*. George and

Marianne were in Dallas by now, checking out Big Tex at the Texas State Fair Grounds, and would be home from their Texas vacation in less than a week.

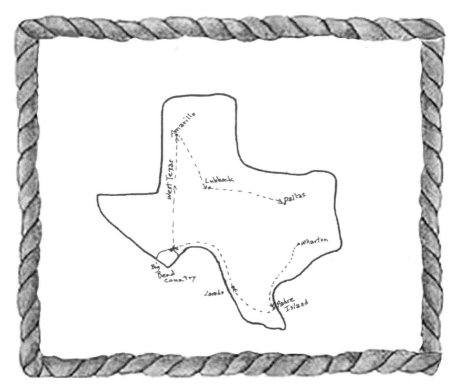

After the first few days of looking for Sugar, one day rolled into the other. The pups were more **subdued** than they were when they first came to visit Grandma Noel. They didn't ask about their mom as often, but thoughts of her still filled the back of their little minds.

Noel was more than **adequate** to the task of caring for and entertaining her grandpups. In a way, the experience helped her relive the days when her own pups had just been weaned. With all the chickens and fine feathered creatures she had met on the farm, she had an ample supply of stories to tell until George and Marianne came back from their vacation for their family of dogs.

Farmer Gabe and Miss Lizzy and Junior had done everything they could do to get Sugar back from whoever had dognapped her. They had filed a report with the sheriff and put an announcement on the local trading post on the radio. Junior had put her picture up in all the grocery stores and washateria's all over town.

They even offered a reward for information concerning her whereabouts. They didn't tell their son and daughter-in-law about the incident because they didn't want to ruin their trip around the Lone Star State. Since they didn't know what else to do, they prayed and asked the Lord to take care of the dog and give her a safe return.

Cowboy didn't chase the neighbor's cows like he used to and Barker only barked when a strange car drove up in the driveway. Punkin wagged her tail for just a few quick swishes when Grandma Noel came to tell them stories. Teddy Bear just lay around all day and didn't even move when Farmer Gabe asked him to ride in the truck. Midnight Star still napped all day, but her dreams were about the good old days when her mom was with them. Bingo tried to figure out a way to find their mom and bring her back home.

Noel just hated seeing all of her grandchildren *down in the dumps* like that, so she called them all together after all the people had gone inside and started her next tale. That night she introduced the gang to the stories about Saddleback, Arky's son.

Grandma Noel began the story. "Farmer Gabe and Miss Lizzy never knew how many chicks old Arky *sired*, but they could tell for sure that Saddleback was one. His head didn't look like his dad, but he was built with big muscles. Although he was mostly white, he had a yellow-brown streak across the top of his upper back and wings, kind of like a saddle. He could have won a contest for 'Mr. Chicken of the Universe' if there had been such a thing.

But in spite of his good looks, there was more to Saddleback than met the eye because he was a genuine survivor!"

"What's a survivor, Grandma?" Bingo wanted to add a new word to his vocabulary.

Noel patiently explained, "A survivor is someone who

can live through many bad circumstances. They may be in danger, but it doesn't have to mean that they are going to die because of it. I know you are just pups, but I'm quite sure you've heard stories that *cats have nine lives*. For some reason, they seem to be more durable than us *canines*. Saddleback was like that because he was headed for danger several times and yet he always escaped by the *skin of his teeth*."

"Grandma, is our mamma a survivor?" Punkin and Teddy Bear questioned her at the same time.

Noel thought carefully before answering. "She just might be. When she was just a pup and we still lived in the city, someone ran over her leg with their car and she had to have it fixed. When it was all healed up, a neighbor's dog got loose and took a bite out of her ear, but she healed up from that, too. And one time she had a bad stomach virus, just couldn't eat anything and God healed her from that sickness, too. Yes, I would have to say she is a survivor, indeed."

The pups seem to have a new glimmer of hope, then Grandma Noel went on with the story. "Saddleback had a lot of times when he was a survivor, too. The first time, he was one of many young roosters that seemed to be abusive to Old Roo and too engrossed in courting the young ladies. There had gotten to be so many teenage boy chickens that the farmer and his wife decided they needed to eliminate some and Saddleback was on the list. One by one, wild young Leghorns and other young roosters went to the Hanging Tree. Junior and his older brothers did the dirty work of beheading them, while Miss Lizzy had the hot water ready to pluck them, then gut them"

"Ewwww! Gross!"Punkin and Midge were thoroughly disgusted at the thought of the killing spree, but their brothers perked their ears up to hear more.

"One of the boys went chasing after Saddleback and caught him, but Saddleback must have known what was up, 'cause he fought back with all he was worth. He skedaddled to safety in the barn where nobody could touch him."

Even Bingo had to laugh when he pictured that scared bird running to safety.

Noel chuckled, too, then shared more of the story. "Another time, the boys tried again to cull out some of the young crowers. Junior used nets to catch them, then loaded the scared birds into cages to take them to a pet store to sell them. Once more they caught Saddleback and again, with super-chicken strength, Arky's son escaped the clutches of death.

He lived in peace for a while, but then one day Miss Lizzy got the hair-brained idea that she could catch him while he was entertaining a lady friend. Just as she grabbed him by the tail feathers, his adrenalin started flowing and it was almost like he let his tail feathers go, like a lizard sheds its tail when it is endangered. This time Miss Lizzy was the one who had a handful of feathers and needed a rest from going on a *wild goose chase* for a chicken."

Cowboy sat up straight now, his eyes alive with the excitement of remembering the time he caught a lizard and it did that very same thing. Meanwhile, Bingo had to ask for the meaning of another big word. "Grandma, tell me what adrenaline is."

Grandma Noel gave her final vocabulary lesson for the evening. "Adrenaline," she said, "is something your body produces that gives you extra strength just when you need it.

Like if you were outside and a mean, strange dog came into the yard, adrenalin would help you run away real fast, much faster than you would run if you weren't scared."

"Oh, I know," said Cowboy, "like the way I run in the pasture when the bull turns to chase me!"

"That's exactly what I mean," smiled Grandma Noel. Then she told the rest of the tale. "Finally, Miss Lizzy decided that he must be destined to live, so she never set traps for him again. She got to where she enjoyed watching him up on the fence post crowing, just like his daddy had done. In fact, he took over the chicken yard that had been his daddy's **domain**. He liked having control of the chicken house, but he never did quite trust people again.

"Like kingdoms come and go, Saddleback's kingdom fell, too. Miss Lizzy thinks maybe all the frights from earlier in life may have taken their toll. As he got older, he slowed down and seemed very disinterested in everything, even his lady friends. Needless to say, Miss Lizzy and I were not surprised to see him totally slowed down one morning inside the chicken house, **dead as a doornail**. Saddleback was one of the few fowls to die a natural death here on our little acre.

"When I wander around the premises now, I see all kinds of up and coming white roosters with brownish yellow stripes across their backs and I know that in spite of his untimely death, Saddleback lives on in the lives of his **progeny**."

Just after the moon came up in the sky outside and just before the clock struck nine in the house, the pups closed their weary little eyes. And Grandma Noel hoped in her doggy heart that her daughter, Sugar, was a survivor, too, like Saddleback.

'Psalm 17:13, KJV
Arise, O LORD, disappoint him, cast him down:
deliver my soul from the wicked,which is thy sword:

The Andrews Sisters

George and Marianne were in Texarkana where they checked out the Texas Arkansas border as part of their two-week vacation tour of Texas. Farmer Gabe and Miss Lizzy, George's parents, were taking care of their dog, Sugar, and her six pups while they were gone. On the third day of their visit, some *fiend* kidnapped Sugar from the front yard. The family continued their search to find the lost dog before the young couple came back to take her and the little ones home. Noel, the farmer's little terrier dog who was also Sugar's mother, came to the rescue by taking care of the pups while the search continued.

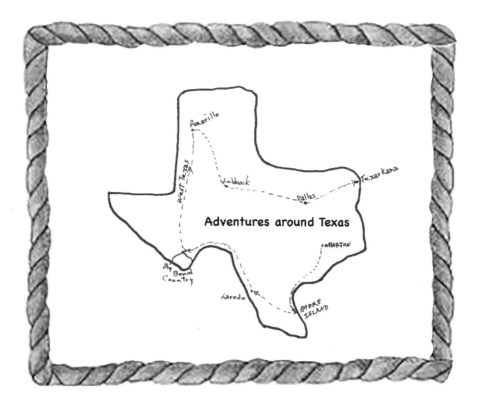

Another day passed with no news of Sugar. Some people say, "No news is good news," but Farmer Gabe and Miss Lizzy were beginning to wonder. The little grandma doggie Noel was keeping the grandpups entertained, but she was concerned about her daughter's well-being as well. Even though the pups behaved themselves, Noel was beginning to feel her age by having to keep up with this *rambunctious* group. Daytime was easy because there were so many things to occupy their attention. Cowboy and Barker found all kinds of places to investigate and critters to chase after. Teddy Bear started riding in the trailer on the lawnmower when Junior cut the grass. Bingo tried to figure out how things worked and the two girls found a sweet kitten from the next farm who wanted to be friends with them. But night time was a ***horse of a different color***.

Even though Noel was a great storyteller, she wondered how many more stories she could come up with before the pups had to go to their home with George and Marianne, possibly without their mom. This was the fifth night of their separation and she hoped the ordeal would come to an end soon with the return of Sugar. The people had already gone in the house for the night, so Noel and the pups were left outside to sleep in the doghouse in the yard as usual. Although she didn't complain, Noel really missed the nice, cool, air-conditioned house. It was a sultry night, like one of those you find in the Texas Gulf Coast during the long, hot days of summer. The half-full moon was shining through wispy clouds that sailed by on starlit seas. It was time for Noel to get the pups ready for bed.

With all the skill of ***Aesop***, Noel began her next tale.

"Once upon a time, not too long after the family moved to 'God's Little Acre,' Junior started raising chicks for a 4-H project for the county fair. When fair time came, most of the grown chickens were sold or went to some relative's dinner table to be chicken and dumplings or some equally delicious dish. But there were three of them that Miss Lizzy and Farmer Gabe were going to raise for laying the next generation of fat little fowl. Farmer Gabe liked them so well that he was the one to come up with an appropriate name for them. He scratched his head and he thought, and he thought. Then it finally dawned on him that the pullets should be Patty, Maxine, and Laverne, the 'Andrews Sisters' like the family that sang and danced together in the '30s and '40s."

"Grandma, what are pullets and why did he give them names like that? What were the real Andrews sisters like?" Punkin and Midge were curious about the pullet's namesakes.

As always, Grandma Noel tried to explain. "Pullets are

chicks that are almost all grown up and ready to lay eggs. The real Andrews Sisters were ladies that entertained soldiers back in the days of the war that Grandpa Johnny fought in. They would go to places where the soldiers were and sing and dance for them. I heard Farmer Gabe tell Miss Lizzy how entertaining it was to watch those three roly-poly pullets and so he gave them their special names.

"Those three little hens were *birds of a feather that always flocked together*, even when they did precision running. Sometimes all three of them would spread their wings out at the same time like they were going to fly. Their running and waddling was a sight to see, especially as they grew bigger. I've always tried to be prim and proper, but not them! In all my days, except when I had that back problem, I never was as undignified as those fat butterballs, but when they saw the farmer's wife bringing feed out for all of them, especially old bread that she bought just for the chickens, they spread their purty white wings and practically flew to meet her. They were as disproportioned as a bumblebee and the law of Aerodynamics did not work in their behalf."

Wouldn't you know it? Bingo had to ask what aerodynamics meant. After a quick lesson on how things should be proportioned just right in order to fly, Noel went on.

"These girls were hatched in the spring, round about March. By the time August rolled around, Maxine, Patty, and Laverne were fully grown and fat as all get out. They were so fat that they couldn't take the sweltering summer sun. Don't you know, that's why I always tell you to stay in the shade on a hot afternoon and drink lots of water?

"First, Maxine had a heat stroke, then Patty met her demise, and finally only Laverne was left. She tried to stay cool by standing in the middle of a water pan, but she couldn't stay there all day and keep up her feeding schedule, too.

"The 100-degree temperatures almost took her out on several occasions, but Farmer Gabe and Miss Lizzy took quick action and doused her with the water hose. Another time, she almost passed out, then the farmer himself held her beak open and tried to force water down her *gullet*. Then there was the time, she did pass out and Farmer Gabe became a paramedic doing CPR on the poor thing. It was a pitiful sight for sure!"

"Grandma, what is CPR? Is Farmer Gabe really a paramedic? How did that save Laverne?" Bingo burst forth with another flood of questions.

"Slow down, child! I can only answer one thing at a time." With the patience of *Job*, Noel described how CPR means pumping on someone's heart in order to get it started again and that paramedics are the people who are kind of like doctors who go in ambulances to help people who are really sick. Then it was time to wind down for the night by finishing the rest of the story.

Noel *reminisced* once more. "They saved her time and again, but the day came that the farmer and Miss Lizzy were both gone from sunup til almost sundown. On that sizzling hot afternoon, Miss Lizzy came home and found that the pullet had perished. This was one time it didn't pay to **count their eggs before they were laid**. And they missed out on having the chicken and dumplings, too!"

"Grandma, now we're sad again. Why do you always tell us sad stories?" All the pups were confused by this recurring turn of events.

"Now, babies, listen to me and listen to me well. Yes, there is a lot of death in my stories, but don't you see that every time there was trouble, Farmer Gabe and Miss Lizzy tried to help the animals if they could. They are here to take care of us and they do the best they can. Sometimes things work out okay, sometimes they don't, but they're our friends. Now if they care for their chickens like that, don't you think they care for us like that, too? And that includes your mom. And if there is any way possible for them to find her, with the good Lord's help, they will do it. So, we have to trust the Lord, too, and not give up hope."

That was enough to satisfy the pups for the night and they all soon fell into a restful sleep dreaming of what it might be like when they could finally reunite with their long-lost mom.

Proverbs 12:10, KJV

A righteous man regardeth the life of his beast: but the tender mercies of the wicked are cruel

The Old Girls

There weren't too many days left before George and Marianne, Farmer Gabe and Miss Lizzy's son and daughter-in-law were to return from their tour of Texas. Because they were already in Nacogdoches, they visited Stephen F. Austin University. They were almost back to his parent's home on the Texas Gulf Coast. They would be anxious to take their dog Sugar back home along with her six pups. What they didn't know was that while Farmer Gabe and Miss Lizzy were taking care of their pets, Sugar had been stolen from the front yard of the farm house and Noel, the farmer's little dog and Sugar's mother, had been dogsitting for the little ones. Junior, George's youngest brother and the farmer's son, had put posters up all over town and Miss Lizzy had advertised in the paper and on the radio for her safe return.

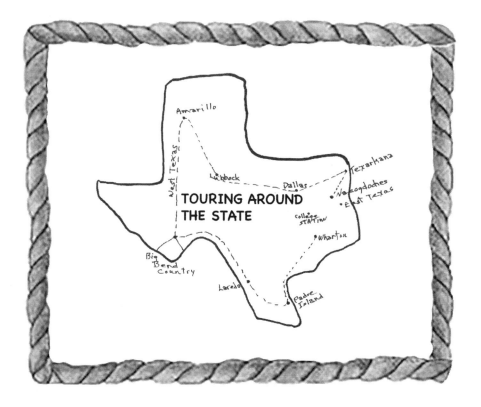

It seemed like the days just got hotter and hotter as the **dog days of summer** continued. Noel had heard Farmer Gabe and Miss Lizzy talking a few times about possible clues to finding Sugar, but to no avail. Sometimes the phone would ring and they would hurry to go see the people who had called only to come back home empty handed. It was hard to stay upbeat and cheerful when they weren't getting what they prayed for. But they never gave up hope. That gave Noel the background for her next story… to have faith and trust in God.

This time, it was a clear night with stars as bright as diamonds and the bright yellow moon was just a little bigger than it was the night before. It was still hot, but a gentle Texas breeze blew in from the southern gulf as the night progressed. As the pups and their grandma stretched out on the soft carpet grass, Noel began her next episode.

"You know, I'm a *Bible*-believing dog because I was healed by God's touch a few years ago, but I never knew chickens could be healed by God, too!" Grandma asked the pups if they remembered her story about her broken back.

"Wow, Grandma! How could we forget?! That was a great story!" all the pups yapped in agreement.

"Well, children, let me tell you about a time that God healed a bunch of chickens. Miss Lizzy had started her chicken venture with ten chickens she bought from a feed store, and they were doing quite well. But one night, some ***ravenous*** creature came and ***wreaked havoc*** with them. Seems like most of the evil that happens, even to chickens, comes in the shadows of the night. The people and I heard crowing about 2 o'clock one morning and we all thought that was rather unusual. But the next day, we found dead chickens all over the place, more victims of dogs on the loose. Makes me ashamed to be part of the same species! Only the

Bad Rooster and two of his girlfriends had survived the slaughter.

"Is that when they got healed, Grandma? Did the dead chickens come back alive?" Punkin tried to get ahead of the story.

"No, no, baby girl. That's what caused Miss Lizzy to want more chickens. She was not very happy, not after all the work she had put into those hens.

But not to fear, she had a solution to her problem. After she heard an ad on KULP radio Trading Post that someone had chickens for sale, Miss Lizzy called and bought 10 more chickens, five white leghorns and five red Plymouth rocks. She brought those girls home on a warm afternoon in September and settled them in the silver hen house.

The next two days, she found three eggs and that was all. She thought that once they got adjusted to their new surroundings, they would begin laying, so she kept feeding them and talking to them and looking for eggs every day."

"Did she really talk to them, Grandma? That's silly!" Teddy Bear offered his unsolicited opinion.

Bingo defended Miss Lizzy. "You duffus! We're dogs and she talks to us, too!".

"Ooops, I forgot!" Teddy Bear was ashamed of his mistake and all of his brothers and sisters were making fun of him now.

"Sweeties, if you don't behave, I'll stop the story right now!"

The pups straightened up immediately after her reprimand,

so the story continued.

"September turned into October, and still no eggs. Miss Lizzy was aggravated, to put it mildly, that she had been sold old hens.

How could that woman lie about these chickens being young? October became November, and the wait continued. Now she was really upset and even considered taking the chickens back and getting a refund.

Then December came, and Miss Lizzy was so discombobulated that she was ready to just give the girls back, forget the money, and just get on with what few others she had.

And then came January…"

"Grandma, does 'discombobulated' mean that she was really, really angry and didn't know what to do?" Bingo was putting the word clues together.

"That's exactly what it means! You are such a smart pup to have figured that out all by yourself. Finally, Miss Lizzy settled down and thought to herself, 'Here I have all these hens and I haven't even prayed about them! So, I guess I better make things right and pray right now.' So, she prayed out loud from her heart, just like this…

"Father, I thank You for these old hens and I thank You for

allowing me to have them. Lord, would You please bless them? I know they are old, but You let **Abraham's wife Sarah** become fertile in her old age. Could You, would You, let them become fertile in their old age as well? And I thank You in Jesus' name."

"I guess I better explain fertile…for chickens, it means to be able to lay eggs, or for other animals to have babies." Noel knew her little word specialist would be trying to figure out the definition for that new word if she didn't help him out a little.

"Now you're not going to believe this, and I wouldn't believe it either if I hadn't had a miracle of my own, but Missus prayed that prayer every day for just about two weeks and then the miracle came….she finally found eggs. She was so happy that she shouted "Hallelujah! Thank you, Jesus!"

Well, they were 'Old Girls' all right, but they became fertile like Sarah. And they stayed fertile for all the rest of their days.

"GRANDMA!" all the pups barked together, "they didn't die this time!" and the pups smiled and wagged their tails as the bright moon looked down on them with a smile as big as Texas and Grandma Noel gave each one a good night kiss with her wet, red doggie tongue.

Hebrews 11:11, KJV

Through faith also Sara herself received strength to conceive seed, and was delivered of a child when she was past age, because she judged Him faithful who had promised.

Guineas Galore

Grandma Noel had been entertaining her grandpups with stories about chickens on God's Little Acre for the last seven days. Her owners, Farmer Gabe and Miss Lizzy, had been taking care of their son and daughter-in-law's dog, Sugar, and her babies while the young couple was on a tour of Texas vacation. On the third day of caring for the pets, Sugar was stolen from their front yard. The farmers had spent all of their time and energy since that day trying to find her. They hoped that she would be home before they had to tell George and Marianne that their dog was nowhere to be found.

Day eight arrived but Sugar did not. The pups didn't ask about her much anymore, although you could tell she was *out of sight*, but she was not *out of mind*. Farmer Gabe and Miss Lizzy seemed to be answering phone calls all day and running errands, even after dark. Something was brewing, but Noel didn't know what. She kept her vigil of watching the pups, even though it was hard on her old bones. How could she have forgotten how much energy it took to be a mother? Junior had said George and Marianne would come to take the pups home in a couple of days. As much as she loved the little rascals, she would be glad for a rest. All of this activity made her glad that she wasn't fertile like Sarah in this stage of her life. In the meantime, however, she stayed faithful to her task of caring for Sugar's babies.

It was getting harder and harder to come up with something new because she had told so many stories already. Now that the moon was getting fuller, the pups were getting antsier. She knew she needed fresh ammo in the storytelling department. But when the pups gathered around her outside of the doghouse. Noel was transformed into the story dog once more…

"Sometimes I just have to wonder what Miss Lizzy is thinking about when she adds to her collection of feathered friends. Seems like ever since her older young 'uns left home, she spends her food budget on a feed bill for poultry, dogs, and goats. Well, since my stories now are about chickens and such, the next story is about how she got started raising *guineas*. I know- that is a strange sounding name, but it goes for a strange looking bird from Africa. Their bodies are kind of square, their necks are long, their heads are small, their squawking hurts my ears, and they love to eat bugs all day long."

Cowboy and Teddy Bear got all excited because they had chased the *guinea* just that day. And he had chased them in return. Papa G didn't like any of the animals messing with him and he let them know it.

"Back when Miss Lizzy brought those two guineas home from the feed store with Arkie and Princess, she didn't know what she was getting in to. Papa G and Mama G ran around the whole yard just like they owned it and they were always together. Miss Lizzy never did figure out which one said something like 'Bob White, Bob White,' and which one said 'JerrRee, Jerr Ree.'

"It was September when I first made their acquaintance. She bought these two speckled specimens when they were almost grown. They were friendly enough with me, but I saw them torture some of the other creatures around here. The deadly duo was especially cruel to Arkie before he went through his metamorphosis."

"Grandma, you used a big word again. What is meta-morphosis?"

"Why, baby that just means changing from one shape to another, like a butterfly lays eggs, they turn into caterpillars and make cocoons, then they turn into butterflies. That is called metamorphosis and Arkie kind of went through a metamorphosis himself when he went from being a strange looking chicken to being the best rooster on this here farm. Now do you understand?"

"Yeah, Grandma, kind of like those little tadpoles turned into frogs down at the pond." Barker showed that he really did understand, as did the rest of the group." And that's when I like to chase them!"

Noel smiled and went on with her story. "Those guineas would gang up on him and start pecking at his tail feathers like he was an alien being and the poor old boy would just run in circles trying to escape their hostility. I just never could figure out why they acted so hateful since Arkie never was mean to them. I've always been kind and loving, but my excellent behavior never did rub off on those two *scalawags*."

Punkin and Midnight Star joined in the conversation now. "Why were they so mean, Grandma? Didn't their mommy teach them to be nice like our mommy taught us?"

"Sweetie, that meanness just seems to be in their nature. Just like some dogs are sweet and cuddly like all of you, some other kinds of dogs are really vicious and will do bad things to hurt other animals and people too. The guineas just don't know how to be nice to the other birds, so everyone else is kind of scared of them. But you know Miss Lizzy- she liked them anyway".

"When March rolled around, Miss Lizzy noticed that Papa G was a onesome instead of part of a twosome. She couldn't figure out where his lady friend had disappeared to. Later that day, Mama G came out of the bushes and Miss Lizzy and Farmer Gabe found out that the guinea family was about to increase in size. The little mommy-to-be had a nest hiding under an old piece of concrete and she was doing her best to take care of it day and night, so the mystery was solved.

"April came. It was almost 28 days since she started nesting and the farmers came to check on her every day."
It was time for another question from the little ones. "Grandma," said Midge, "I thought you said it took only three weeks for eggs to hatch."

"Yes, baby. You have been paying close attention! It does take only twenty-one days if it's chicken eggs, but guinea eggs take four weeks instead. I guess that's because the guineas are a little bit bigger."

"One dismal night a horrific rainstorm soaked our area and some hungry *ogre* decided to give Mama G a chance to be part of his menu. Of course, she fought for her life and especially fought for the safety of her eggs, but it just was not to be. I always wondered where the big brave papa was when all of this was going on. He must have *flown the coop* for that night! The next morning, Miss Lizzy found the eggs but no sign of little mama.

"She was like Princess, hiding her nest, wasn't she, Grandma?" Bingo knew how the two stories were related. "She hid her nest, then she died taking care of it."

"Bingo, baby, that is exactly right. And Miss Lizzy tried to save her eggs, too. She thought maybe there was still hope for them, so she went *flittin'* on down to the feed store and spent a small fortune on that incubator that I told you about in the story of Princess. The storekeeper assured her that it really would hatch out the eggs, so Miss Lizzy carried it on home. Miss Lizzy and Farmer Gabe got that contraption all set up and it really did work, for at least some of the eggs. They ended up with three tiny little guineas that Miss Lizzy and Farmer Gabe kept in a bird cage in the house until they were big enough to fend for themselves. I tell you the truth, those keets, -- that's the real name for baby guineas,—were treated like royalty.

"The day finally came when it was time to let the babies go. Like a mother sending her kiddos off to college, Miss Lizzy was *reluctant* to let her prize guinea babies move off into the chicken house dorm, but she knew she couldn't keep them caged in the people's home forever.

"There was another time this hard-headed woman raised guineas and she did have better results, but those crazy birds weren't very smart. Some of them flew into the fenced-in back yard and the rude, crude doggies back there thought they came to be lunch.

Others tried to race the cars zooming down the road in front of our house and ended up in a road kill café somewhere for buzzards. With all the dozens of guineas she raised, Miss Lizzy finally ended up with one lonely male. He gets along, all right, but he sure is lonesome without love."

"We have love, don't we Grandma?" the pups barked in chorus.

"That you do, you precious bunch of mongrels. That you do!" and she moved into the dog house and the pups followed her, then they all curled up together for a good night's rest.

Ecclesiastes 4:10.11, KJV

For if they fall, the one will lift up his fellow: but woe to him that is alone when he falleth; for he hath not another to help him up. Again, if two lie together, then they have heat: but how can one be warm alone?

Tag Team Olympics

Noel could feel something in the air, but she wasn't sure just what. She had been taking care of her daughter Sugar's pups for the last ten days because Sugar had been stolen from the family's front yard. Farmer Gabe and Miss Lizzy were starting to smile again for the first time since Sugar had been taken. They were hoping to get the dog back before their son George and his wife Marianne came back from traveling around the great state of Texas.

Their last stop before they arrived home would be College Station to check out an Aggie scrimmage game. The farmers had been taking care of the dog family for George and Marianne, their son and daughter in law, and had not told them yet about the dognapping. Farmer Gabe and Miss Lizzy and Junior, their youngest son, had been praying for a safe return. Although nine days had already gone by, there had not been much to go on. But tonight seemed to be different and Noel would soon find out why.

It was the night before George and Marianne were to return from their vacation. Farmer Gabe and Miss Lizzy were talking excitedly on the phone and it sounded like good news. Noel just happened to be in the house for a change.(That hadn't happened much since the pups came to stay.) She got excited herself when she heard them say, "Yes, that sounds just like Sugar. Yes, we'll meet you tomorrow evening at the courthouse square. You will be rewarded for helping us to get her back. Thank you so much for calling to let us know you found her"

Noel, being the intelligent dog that she was, knew this meant her pup sitting days were almost done for this time around. Oh, how badly she wanted to **spill the beans**! But she knew that sometimes, things go wrong, so she kept that information to herself. She had a new energy about her when bedtime came and the pups couldn't help but notice.

"Grandma, you look different? Did Miss Lizzy give you a bath today?" that was the first thing Punkin could think of that might make a change.

"You must have had a long nap!" Midnight Star thought of how that always made her feel better.

"No, she must have had more exercise," Cowboy and

Barker remembered that they always felt much better they felt after running all around the barnyard.

"Grandma, did Farmer Gabe take you for a ride to town in the truck?" even Teddy Bear knew something was different. Bingo seemed to have an insight the others missed."Grandma, did you hear something about our momma?"

Noel smiled and *evaded* the questions. It was hard not to *let the cat out the bag* and blurt out the real reason for her *new lease on life*, but she made herself *mute* on the subject. With renewed vigor, with an almost full moon shining in the heavens, Noel began what she hoped was her last story for this visit.

"You have heard me tell several times about the young roosters. Those boys were an embarrassment to me as a refined lady, but they were a terror to all the young hens and old hens alike. When their testosterone started flowing, there was no stopping them!Seems like when one of them picked a lady friend to go courting with, all of his brothers and friends thought that was the lady they needed to court, too"

"Grandma, you use too many big words. What is testosterone?" the innocence of childhood came through in Bingo's question.

"When boys start to grow up, God gives them something to help them become daddies. People call it testosterone and all these young roosters wanted to become daddies, too." Noel tried her best not to stay on the subject about what happened to the young roosters.

"You see, these young upstarts would be out eating grasshoppers or pill bugs or whatever, then one of them would catch the sight of a purty pullet out of the corner of his eye. Now, we know what teenaged boys do when they see a sweet young thing—they try to impress her.

These youngsters were no different. So his buddies thought, "If that little lady is good enough for him, she's good enough for me, too!" Then the race was on. When the girl figured out that she was the target of unwanted attention, she would run with all she was worth to try to find a place of safety, but usually to no avail.

"First, the instigator would let the hen know he was interested. He would spread out his wing to the ground, then squawk and dance in a circle around his chick. Next, he would whisper sweet nothings in her ear whether she liked him or not. It was thoroughly disgusting! Then his friends took notice and went running and knocked him out of the way. Before you knew it, five or six of those **scalawags** had made romantic advances to the same cute hen. It wasn't so bad in fall and winter, but spring time and summer brought real meaning to learning about the birds and the bees.

Punkin had to ask a question now. "Were they trying to dance with her, Grandma?"

"Baby, it kind of looked that way, but I'm not sure that's what he was trying to do. Miss Lizzy used these occasions to her advantage when it came time to decrease the rooster population. Whenever she was close enough to one who was trying to impress his lady friend, she would just reach down and grab him because he was so preoccupied with the love of his life for that minute. Of course, he put up a fuss, but he learned a lesson the hard way… never be so preoccupied with other things that you don't keep your eyes open for danger.

"It was bad enough what with all the trouble they caused their girlfriends, but it was downright humiliating what they did to senior citizen men of the chicken community. Miss Lizzy and Farmer Gabe noticed it first when they ganged up on Old Roo. They took sheer delight in aggravating the living daylights out of him. Now, I wasn't a real fan of Roo, but I just couldn't watch when one of the gang members, then another one, would run and jump to tackle him. First, they would grab hold of his comb with their sharp beaks. Then they would pluck out a mouthful of feathers out of his tail or off of his back. I guess they never learned to respect their elders so they could have a long, fruitful life like it says in the **Bible**. They made that poor old rooster miserable day after day by making sport of him.

Those adolescents were just as bad with Squatty, one of the other roosters Miss Lizzy acquired when she rebuilt her flock of chickens. Squatty was a yellow and black bantam mix with feathery legs and he never ever did any harm to any of the others. You'd have thought he was the worst sinner boy in the world by the punishment these youngsters doled out to him."

"We could never be that mean to each other or anyone else!" All the pups realized the importance of respecting their elders and each other.

Noel commended them proudly. "That is wonderful that you can see how wrong it was for them to be like that. Well, Judgment Day came for the tormentors on several occasions. One time three of Farmer Gabe and Miss Lizzy's sons went on a rooster culling spree. That's when they established the Hanging Tree. The next year, they decided to round up the next generation of crowers and send them down the road to a pet store where some farmers were waiting to purchase new arrivals. We have our suspicions that those roosters ended up as a meal on someone's table. Another year, Farmer Gabe told his friends that he had roosters to give away and to come help themselves. Boy, that thinned them out!"

"Why did they always have to get rid of extra roosters, Grandma? Didn't they like having them around?" The boy pups were beginning to wonder about their own *destinies*.

"Oh, my yes," Grandma explained. "But when people live on a farm, sometimes they have to decide which animals are the best ones to have around, and which ones are only there to cause trouble and to eat up their food. And most times, too many roosters eat up all the grain, but don't do anything to help out around the farm. The farmers keep the hens because they lay eggs, but the roosters just eat all day long and hold crowing contests. Farmer Gabe and Miss Lizzy usually keep a few, but too many roosters cost too much money. But they like having dogs around because we help protect them from intruders."

All the boy pups breathed a sigh of relief. Then they asked Noel to finish her tale.

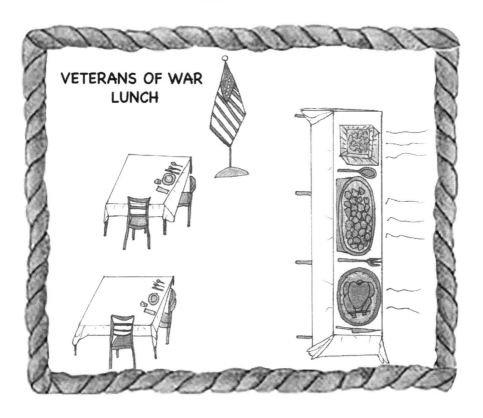

"There was another outlet for excess poultry and that was Grandpa Johnny. Whenever he needed to take food along to one of his *Veterans of Foreign Wars* meetings, he would call Miss Lizzy and make his request…. 'You got any roosters you need to get rid of?' Miss Lizzy would tell Junior and Junior would load up as many as he could, then he delivered them to Grandpa Johnny. Needless to say, when the roosters met Grandpa, that old soldier made sure they met their maker, too. Then he took them into Grandma Geraldine and she turned them into the best chicken and dumplings or chicken spaghetti you ever did sink your teeth into."

"Grandma," said Bingo thoughtfully, "I sure am glad I'm a dog and not a teenage rooster!" All the pups murmured in agreement.

And as Noel gave each pup a lick goodnight, she smiled about the secret that she hoped would be revealed on the morrow.

Deuteronomy 5:16, KJV

Honour thy father and thy mother, as the LORD thy God hath commanded thee; that thy days may be prolonged, and that it may go well with thee, in the land which the LORD thy God giveth thee.

Proverbs 19: 26, KJV

He that wasteth his father, and chaseth away his mother, is a son that causeth shame, and bringeth reproach.

Princess's Progeny
The Stories Come to an End

It was the fourteenth day of George and Marianne's vacation and the eleventh day since Sugar's disappearance. The couple had been to Padre Island, the border town of Laredo, Big Bend National Park and the Panhandle. Their return route took them to Dallas, Texarkana, Nacogdoches, East Texas, and College Station. Soon they would be home with Farmer Gabe and Miss Lizzy so they could pick up their pooches and head to their own home in the city. Noel, Farmer Gabe and Miss Lizzy's dog, knew a secret and her grand pups, Sugar's children, would soon find out...

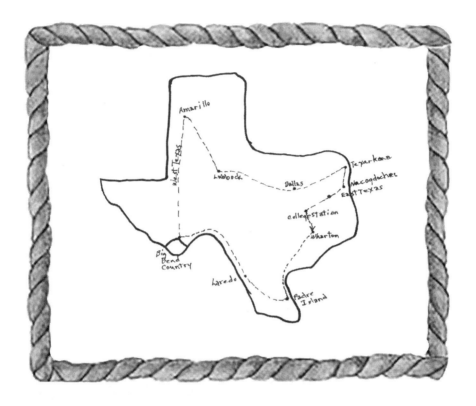

Miss Lizzy was running around the farm *like a chicken with her head cut off* trying to get ready for two big reunions: the first with their son George and his wife Marianne who had been gone for vacation for two weeks, and the second with their dog, Sugar, who had been stolen ten days earlier. She and Farmer Gabe had been taking care of Sugar and her six pups when a dognapper stole her from the front yard of the farmhouse.

Farmer Gabe was doing his share to get the place ready for their return. Sugar's pup, Teddy Bear had been riding around with him all day on the big lawnmower, but he really didn't know what all the commotion was about. Junior had the job of giving all of the pups baths, especially Barker and Cowboy, who had been out rolling in the mud in the neighbor's pasture. Punkin and Midge were fairly clean, but he bathed them anyway and brushed their hair to make their coats glow. Bingo was the only pup who was aware of a change in the atmosphere.

Noel had been harboring a secret since the night before. She had overheard a phone conversation when the people were talking about Sugar's return. Although it was a hard thing to do, she kept it to herself just in case it was a false alarm. It was all she could do to stay cool, calm and collected even though she was about to burst on the inside.

Late that afternoon, after all the pups were cleaned up, Farmer Gabe and Miss Lizzy and Junior went to town. The pups were confused by all the activity and Noel knew they needed to stay clean, so she used this opportunity to tell them a story.

"Punkin, Midge, Cowboy, Barker, Teddy Bear, Bingo, come here quickly." I want to tell you another story."

"Grandma," the shocked pups responded, "It's not even bedtime yet!"

"Oh, I know. But let's let this be a special treat."

With that explanation, the pups settled down and Noel commenced the last of many memorable tales.

"Lookin' back over what I've been tellin' you so far, I see I neglected to tell you about some of Princess's daughters. Most of them turned into really good mothers just like their precious little mom, but one was especially outstanding. Miss Dottie was a black and white speckled hen, not solid black like her mother.

She was well rounded all over and her head feathers were more like a bouffant hairstyle instead of a *Pebbles-like fountain*. But when it came to being a gentle hen, she was top of the line".

"I'm gonna be a good mommy like my mommy," said Punkin.

"I am, too," declared Midnight Star.

"And I'm gonna be a good daddy," said Bingo. Before long, all the boy pups had their chance to say so, too. Noel had to shush them so she could continue the story.

"Dottie started hatching eggs when her first springtime came. Farmer Gabe and Miss Lizzy found her nesting, so they gave her her very own nursery room.

Actually, it was just a chicken pen with a door on it to keep her in and varmints out."

"Miss Marianne gave our mommy a special room like that in our house when we were born," Punkin and Midnight Star could relate to the nursery analogy. They had lived there for the first three weeks of their lives.

"When I had pups, Miss Lizzy and Farmer Gabe gave me a special room, too. It sure was nice to have a place inside the house. Well, anyway, back to Miss Dottie. She was one of the easiest hens to transfer from the barnyard to the maternity ward. Never once did she peck at the people or cause a commotion. When Miss Dottie's eggs started hatching, it just so happened another batch of eggs were cracking open in the incubator. So, you guessed it, Farmer Gabe and Miss Lizzy started giving each newly hatched chick to Miss Dottie and she acted as though it had been there all the time. By the time all the eggs under her and the incubator babies hatched out, she had so many children, she didn't know what to do. But she never failed to take care of each and everyone."

"I liked that story, Grandma, but it was sure short. Tell us more. Your stories are better than barking at lizards on a hot afternoon." All the other pups agreed with Barker.

"I'll even give up my nap if you will tell us another story" Midge was wide awake now.

Cowboy joined in, "I'd rather stay here under the shade tree listening to your stories than go chasing the goats or the cows."

After Punkin and Teddy Bear and Bingo had their say, Noel decided to go for another round. She went on bragging about Princess and her *progeny*.

"Princess was a good mother and she passed on her mothering abilities to almost all of her female offspring. They were so much like her that as soon as they started laying eggs, they became sitters, too. I loved being a mother, but I just can't imagine having five or six sets of little ones, like she did.

"Farmer Gabe and Miss Lizzy noticed an interesting phenomenon once the little ladies grew up. One would start sitting on a batch of eggs, then a day or two later, one of her sisters would join her. She wasn't there just to visit—she wanted to make sure her chickees would be close to her sister's chickees when they hatched. The two little layers would take turns keeping the nest warm. When one went down for a bite to eat, the other would stay on duty *keeping the home fires burning*. Why, at one point in time there were three of the little ladies-in-waiting sitting on shared eggs!

Sure enough, when the eggs were ready, the mommies shared the fuzzy babies just like yours, mine, and ours. I don't know if they knew which babies belonged to which bird by the time all of them hatched out. I'd have to say this was a true picture of sisterly love. Even now Farmer Gabe and Miss Lizzy find hens sharing nests and I think it is indeed a wonderful thing for sisters to dwell in peace together. And that's another reason Princess's children were special"

The pups were still trying to figure out why story time was happening so early in the day, but they weren't about to disrupt the pleasant atmosphere. Noel kept listening for cars and things, but the road was silent. As evening shadows started to fall, she decided to tell one more round.

"The first batch of babies that Princess hatched was the most memorable to Farmer Gabe and Miss Lizzy because they thought it was such a novel idea to be hatching chicks." Noel laughed at the memory. "Every time they heard a new little chirp, they carried on like a couple of first graders with a new toy. It reminded me of how they used to ooooh and aaaaaah at my pups in my younger days. Oh, how I miss those days! Anyway, back to my story…

"One of the first little ones was solid black with a smidgen of a yellow topknot above its head. As time went on, the crested feathers began to get longer, so Miss Lizzy thought, 'Black feathers, long hair, this baby has got to be ELVIS!' As always, she had to give it a name and this time, it was named after the famous entertainer. So she would tell Elvis 'hi' whenever she went to the chicken yard and Elvis would go running to hide.

"When Elvis got older, he never did start crowing, but that didn't bother Miss Lizzy because there were so many others who were exercising their vocal cords. But one day Miss Lizzy found out she made a big mistake. Elvis had been sitting in the hen house and when he moved, Miss Lizzy found a warm egg where he had been setting. It turned out that 'Elvis' was really 'Elvira!'

"Don't know why and I guess it doesn't really matter, but Elvira is probably the only hen descended from Princess that the nesting genes totally skipped. She certainly did lay eggs, but never once did the mothering instinct take hold. She always did seem *nutty as a fruitcake*. And she stayed skittish all the days of her life."

"Grandma, is that the silly looking chicken with hair sprouting all over the top of her head? I always wondered what was wrong with her." Bingo was first to say something. "Well," Grandma replied, "it takes all kinds to **make the world go around**, and chickens like Elvira help make things interesting."

Just about the time they all laughed, Noel heard a car coming and her ears perked up quickly. The pups heard, too, and recognized the sound of George and Marianne's car coming down the road. Soon they would be on their way back to the city, probably without their mom.

118

Suddenly, Farmer Gabe and Miss Lizzy drove up, too, and Junior swung open the back door. The puppies' eyes popped open when they saw their long-lost mother Sugar running to greet them. Junior hurried to open the back gate and a much thinner mamma doggy returned safely to her litter. Their prayers had been answered and the family was reunited. Noel was grateful that her secret had been fulfilled.

All the people were hugging and kissing and just being so glad that there was a happy ending to what could have been a very sad story. As George and Marianne petted Sugar and played with each of the pups, they remarked over and over again how much they had grown in the two weeks while they had been gone. After one final session, they went with Farmer Gabe, Miss Lizzy, and Junior into the house to hear a rundown of all that had happened. There was so much to tell and so little time to tell it!

There was much to tell in the doggy world as well. Sugar was *inundated* with questions about her ordeal. The full moon was rising in the eastern horizon as the litter of pups and Grandma Noel listened to Sugar's story of separation, pain, fear, and complete trust in the God of her mother. With hearts as full of joy as the moon was full of light, the pups and Sugar waited to go home with the young couple. But they would never forget the last two weeks and their stay with Farmer Gabe, Miss Lizzy, and Junior and Grandma Noel and all of her memorable tales from the chicken yard, and the other fowl stories, too.

Isaiah 49:15, KJV

Can a woman forget her sucking child, that she should not have compassion on the son of her womb? Yea, they may forget, yet will I not forget thee

Psalms 133:1 , KJV

Behold, how good and how pleasant it is for brethren to dwell together in unity!

Job 39:17, KJV

God hath deprived her of wisdom, neither hath he imparted to her understanding.

Epilogue

She doesn't rightly know why there was so much dying on this little acre, but Miss Lizzy came to realize that dying is a part of living and the cycle of life goes on even when it seems useless. You see, farm life, even on a little acre, teaches the true concept of Ecclesiastes 3 from the *Bible*:

To everything, there is a season,
and a time to every purpose under the heaven:
A time to be born, and a time to die;
a time to plant, and
a time to pluck up that which is planted;
A time to kill, and a time to heal;
a time to break down, and a time to build up;
A time to weep, and a time to laugh;
a time to mourn, and a time to dance;
A time to cast away stones,
and a time to gather stones together;
a time to embrace,
and a time to refrain from embracing;
A time to get, and a time to lose; a time to keep,

and a time to cast away;

A time to rend,

and a time to sew;

a time to keep silence, and a time to speak;

A time to love, and a time to hate;

a time of war, and a time of peace.

He hath made everything beautiful in his time:

Also, He hath set the world in their heart,

so that no man can find out the work that God maketh from

the beginning to the end.

I said in mine heart, God shall judge the righteous and the

wicked:

for there is a time for every purpose

and for every work.

This hasn't been one of Miss Lizzy's favorite lessons, but it gives her peace to know that of all her seemingly hard setbacks, God is still in His heaven and that He is in charge of all the affairs of men.

Glossary

Prologue

Dognappers—Someone who snatches dogs instead of children.

Rural—Area where people live in the country.

Needle in a haystack—Very hard to find.

Interjected—Said something while other people were talking.

Pray Tell—Please tell me.

Committed—Asked God to keep her safe.

Reluctant—Unwilling to do something.

Noel Tells Tales from the Chicken Yard

Admonished—Scolded in a gentle way.

Spittin' Image—Strong resemblance to someone else.

Euthanasia—Putting to death painlessly.

Perplexed—Confused.

Prognosis—Probable cause of a disease.

Instantaneous—Completed in an instant.

Shenanigans—Mischief.

That Bad Rooster

His Better Half—His wife.

Just a hop, skip, and a jump—Not very far.

Character—Someone who has a very unique personality.

Had Been Around The Barnyard A Few Times—Had a great deal of experience.

Spurs—A stiff sharp extension from a rooster's leg.

Wattles—A fleshly wrinkled fold of skin located under a rooster's beak.

Walk Softly BUT Carry A Big Stick—Walk carefully but be prepared for trouble.

Death's Doorstep—Looked ready to die.

Upset His Apple Cart—Unexpected change in how things are done.

A Taste Of His Own Medicine—Was being treated like he had treated others.

Like An Old Eskimo Going To The Polar Bears–A legend Miss Lizzy had heard that when old Eskimos are ready to die, they go out on the ice floes to be with the polar bears.

Bodacious—Remarkable, gutsy.

Princess, the Dignified Hen

Plumb Tuckered Out—Completely tired.

Guinea—Black and white speckled bird originally from Africa.

Nomers And Misnomers—Names that were good and names that weren't so good.

Grieved—Expressed great sorrow.

Joshin'—Teasing.

Reminisced—Good memories of past experiences.

Gave Up The Ghost—Died.

Scamp—Playful young person.

The Hen That Crowed

Canines—Animals that are part of the dog family.

Surrogate Mother—Someone who takes the place of another.

Tricks Up Her Sleeve—Knew a lot of ways to entertain.

Descendant—Related to a specific ancestor.

Fertility—Ability to produce children.

Harassing—Picking on others, annoying.

Raucous—A lot of noise.

Lock, Stock, And Barrel—Took everything.

King David's Men After Their Beards Were Cut Off—Story from the *Bible* in 2 Samuel 10:4,5.

Saddleback, Arky's Son

Subdued—Quieter than usual.

Adequate—Had more than enough experience.

Down In The Dumps—Sad or discouraged.

Sired—Male parent.

Cats Have Nine Lives—Cats survive many dangerous situations.

Skin Of His Teeth—Just barely escaped.

Wild Goose Chase—Wild search for something unobtainable.

Domain—The area a person is in charge of.

Dead As A Doornail—Completely dead.

Progeny—His children.

The Andrews Sisters

Fiend—A wicked person.

Rambunctious—Full of energy.

Horse Of A Different Color–Something altogether separate and unexpected.

Aesop—A world renown storyteller who was a slave from ancient Greece.

Birds Of A Feather Flock Together—Birds that are like each other tend to stay together.

Gullet—A birds throat.

Job—A very patient man who suffered many calamities.

Count Their Eggs Before They Were Laid—Related to the proverb "don't count your chickens before they are hatched."

The Old Girls

Dog Days Of Summer—The sultry part of summer, usually between July 3 and August 11.

Ravenous—Extremely hungry

Wreaked Havoc—Caused all kinds of trouble

Abraham's Wife Sarah—Lady in the Old Testament who had a baby when she was 90 years old.

Guineas Galore

Out Of Sight And Out Of Mind– A person who is not always around is not always thought about.

Scalawag—A rascal.

Ogre—A mean or cruel animal.

Flown The Coop—Ran away.

Flittin'—Moving lightly and swiftly.

Spill The Beans—To tell a secret to someone who is not supposed to know.

Evaded—Stayed away from.

Let The Cat Out Of The Bag—To tell something that's supposed to be a secret.

New Lease On Life—A new chance to live.

Mute—Chose not to talk.

Destinies—Things that are going to happen in the future.

Veterans of Foreign Wars (VFW)—American men and women who have fought in wars in foreign countries.

Princess Progeny

Like A Chicken With Her Head Cut Off—Running around in a crazy manner.

Pebbles-Like Fountain—A hairstyle like Fred Flintstone's baby daughter Pebbles.

Keep The Home Fires Burning—Taking care of things at home while someone is away.

Nutty As A Fruitcake—Very crazy.

Make The World Go Around—Makes life interesting.

Inundated—Overwhelmed.

About The Author

Elizabeth Dettling Moreno is a mother of five, grandmother of sixteen, great grandmother of seven, and a retired teacher who lives with her youngest son Gabriel in the small country town of Wharton on the Texas Gulf Coast. Gabe, her husband of 39 years, passed away in 2019.

They live on God's Little Acre with their two dogs and a small flock of chickens, but Noel has gone on to her eternal reward. They also have several roosters, two guineas, and a cat. She is a member of Abundant Life Church in Wharton.

Mrs. Moreno is the author of two children's books, *Sancho, The Silly Billy Goat*, and *The Return of Sancho the Not-So-Silly Billy Goat.* She also authored the coloring book *The COVID Pandemic and How the Animals Saved the Day* in April, 2020.

She helped Holocaust survivor Helen Colin write her autobiography, *My Dream of Freedom: From the Holocaust to my Beloved America*.

About The Illustrator

Jeanette Smaistrla Crum is a Texas native of Wharton County. She was raised on a farm in East Bernard, Texas with six brothers and a sister. She is a mother of two boys and one girl. She is blessed with five grandsons and three granddaughters, one great grandson and a great granddaughter. She enjoys her retired life living with her youngest son and family in Liberty Lake, Washington where she discovered a new hobby of acrylic painting and drawing. Her retirement is enjoyable and exciting.